MAY 2017

# Different?
# Same!

Written by **Heather Tekavec**

Illustrated by **Pippa Curnick**

Kids Can Press

We are all different, as different as can be.
Take a quick look — it's easy to see.

I gallop.

ZEBRA

I fly.

BUMBLEBEE

I leap.

RING-TAILED
LEMUR

TIGER

I prowl.

But look closer now ...
We all have STRIPES!

TIGER

I live in the jungle.

WALRUS

I live in the Arctic.

I'm leathery.

I'm shiny.

RHINOCEROS
rainasards

RHINOCEROS
BEETLE

I'm shaggy.

BISON

IMPALA

I'm lean.

But look closer now ...
We all have HORNS!

I'm a fast swimmer.

TURTLE

I'm strong for my size.

RHINOCEROS
BEETLE

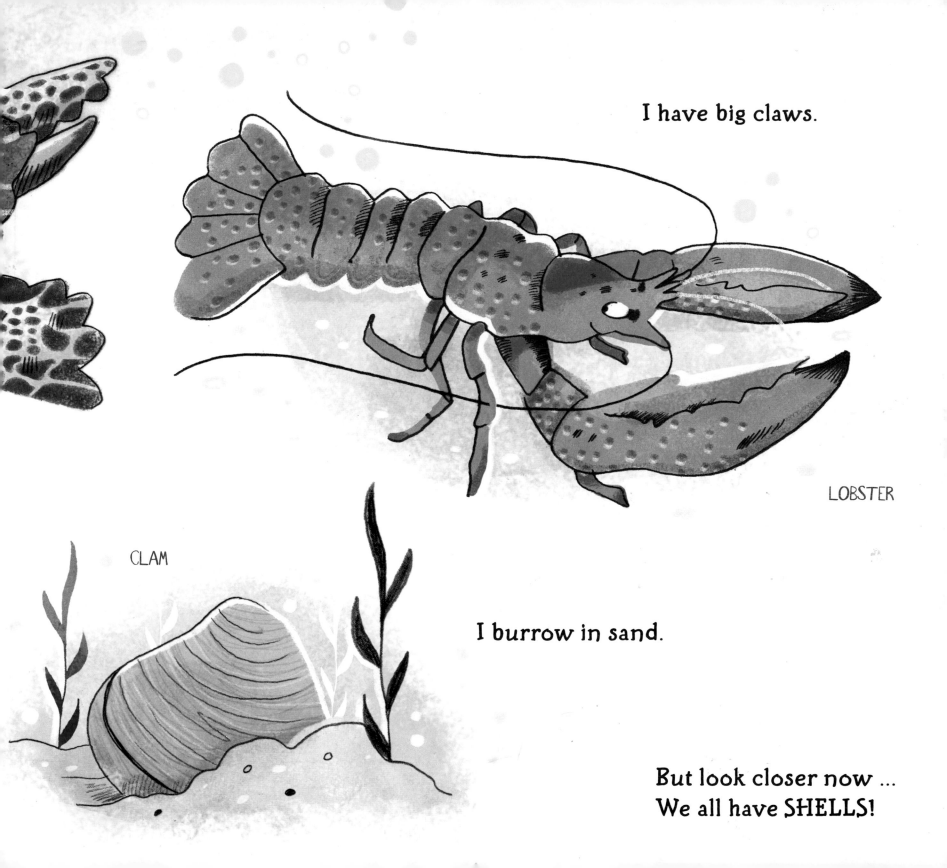

I tunnel underground.

ANT

GRASSHOPPER

I hop through the meadow.

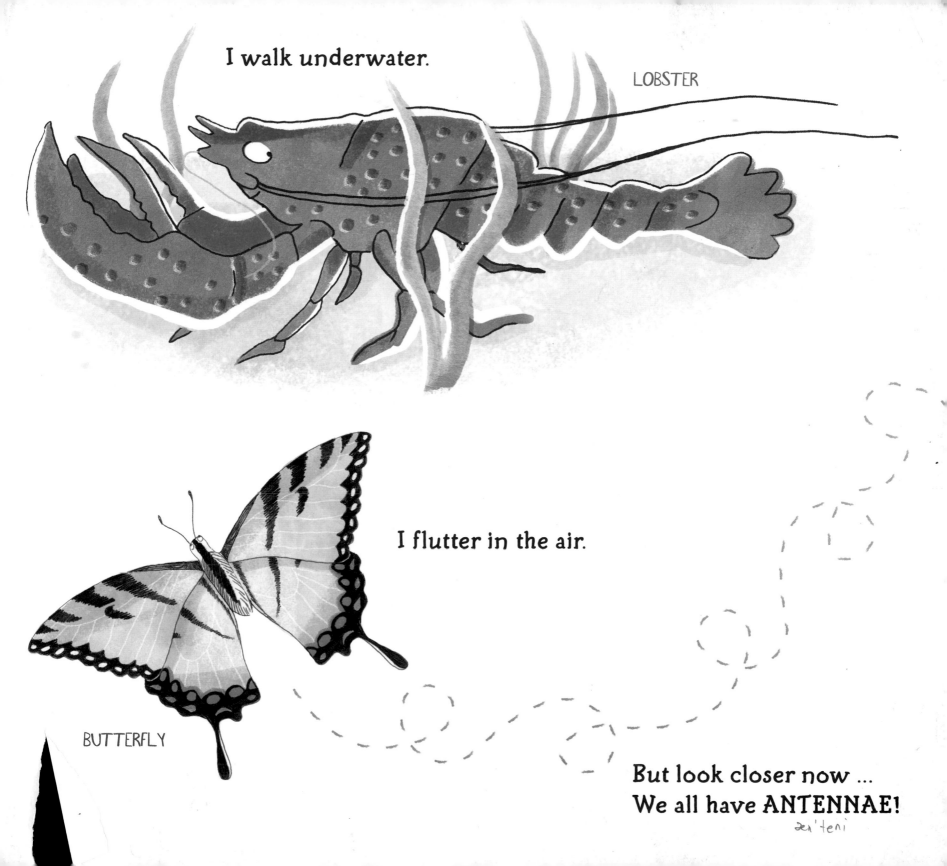

I'm blue.

BLUE JAY

I'm yellow.

BUTTERFLY

I squeak.

BAT

I meow.

CAT

I'm blubbery.

WALRUS

I'm wrinkly.

ELEPHANT

I'm bristly.
bristli 有刚毛

WARTHOG
野猪

NARWHAL

I'm smooth.

But look closer now ...
We all have TUSKS!
长牙 (tʌsks)

LION

I stalk.
瑜著走

HORSE

I race. [res]
競走

I growl.

I hiss.

SNAKE

BEAR

But look closer now ...
We all have FANGS!

CHAMELEON

I perch.

I slither.

SNAKE

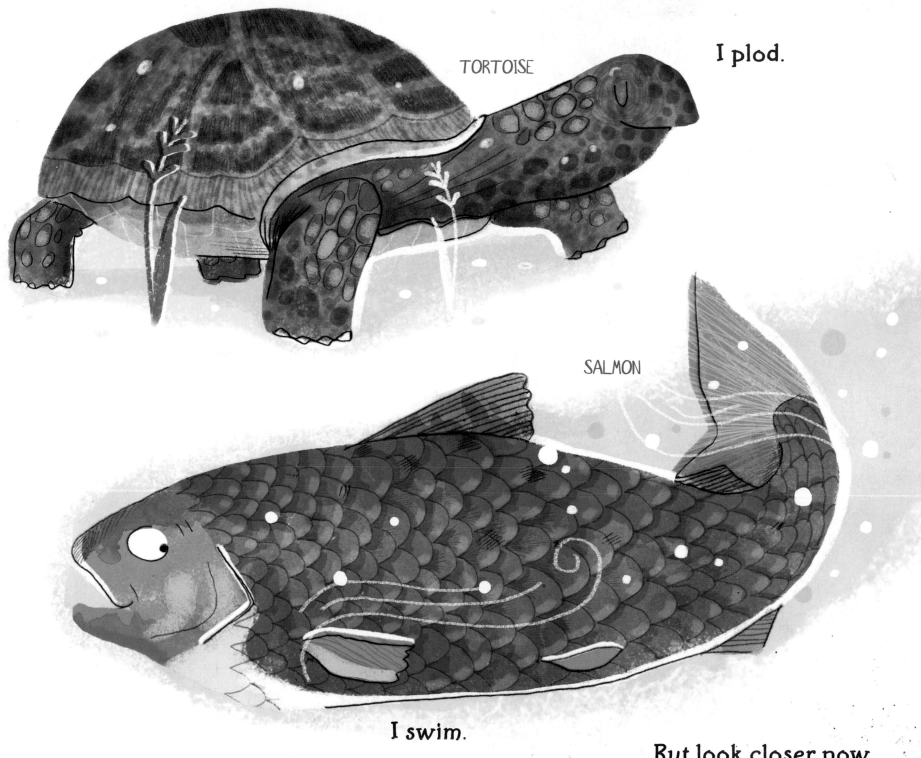

TORTOISE

I plod.

SALMON

I swim.

But look closer now ...
We all have SCALES!

I curl into a ball.

I puff up.

HEDGEHOG

PUFFER
FISH

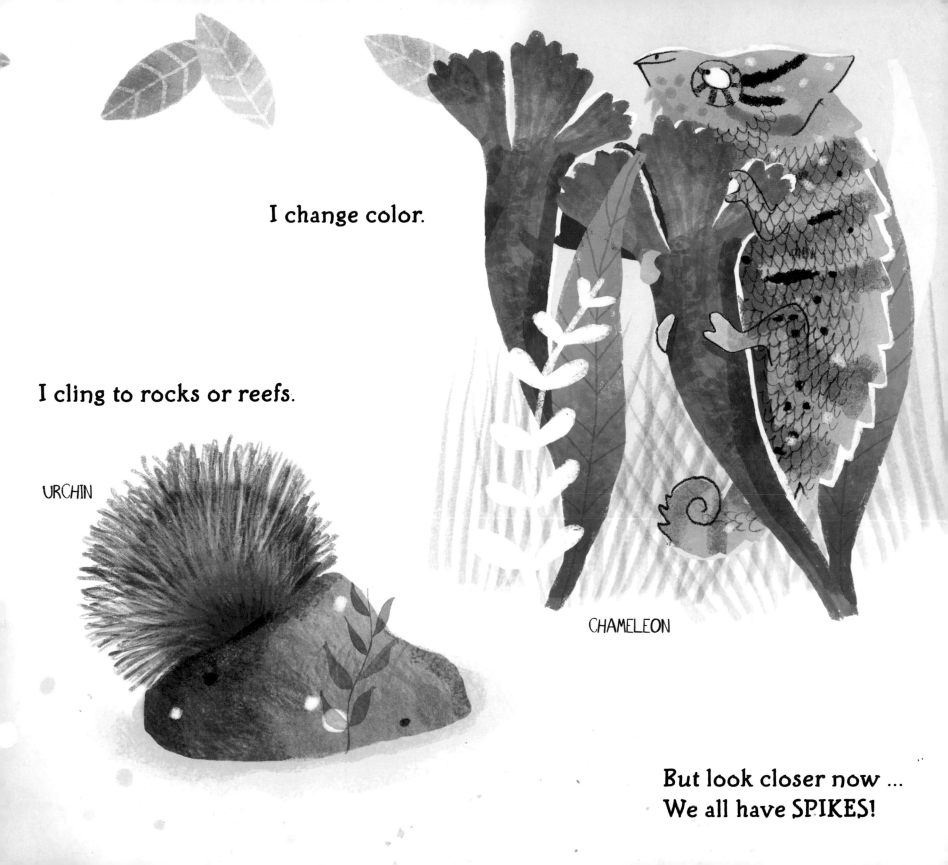

I change color.

I cling to rocks or reefs.

URCHIN

CHAMELEON

But look closer now ...
We all have SPIKES!

I'm sleek.

DOLPHIN

I'm spiky.

PUFFER
FISH

SQUID

I have many arms.

PENGUIN

I'm black and white.

But look closer now ...
We all have FLIPPERS or FINS!

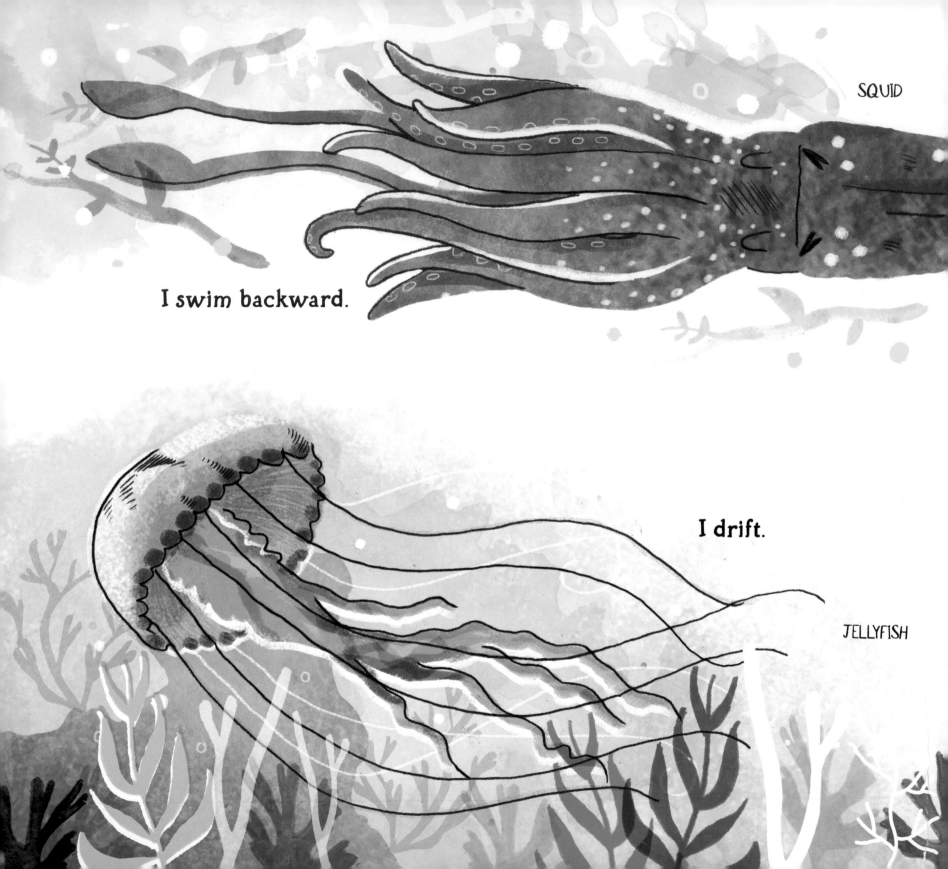

SQUID

I swim backward.

I drift.

JELLYFISH

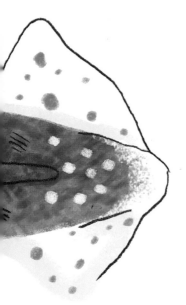

I slide.

SNAIL

I dig.

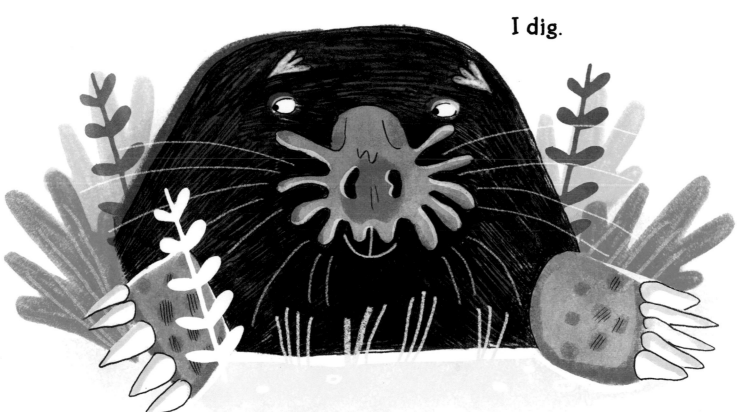

STAR-NOSED MOLE

But look closer now ...
We all have TENTACLES!

If you look close enough, it soon becomes clear ...
we're not as different as we first appear.

How many animals can you find that ...
have spots?
have webbed feet?
are furry?
have beaks?
have no legs?
make good pets?
live in the ocean?
live in the forest?
have six or more legs?
might live in your backyard?
you would NOT like to touch?

# Why Animals Have the Characteristics They Do

## Stripes

Stripes help some animals hide in their surroundings. Zebras hide from enemies, and tigers hide in order to hunt for food. Other animals use stripes to stand out. A bumblebee's bright yellow and black stripes warn all creatures to stay away!

## Whiskers

Whiskers help animals to sense things around them. Animals use their whiskers to tell if a space is too small, if something is getting too close or even which direction a smell is coming from. A walrus uses its whiskers like fingers to find food in the dark.

## Tusks

Tusks are very long teeth that make great tools. Walruses use their tusks to pull themselves up onto the ice. Elephants and warthogs use them to dig and to fight. A narwhal uses its single tusk as a sensor to gather information about its surroundings.

## Manes

Manes are fancy hairdos, warm scarves and protective padding all in one! Horses use their manes to protect them from flies and other biting insects. A lion's mane shows his enemies how strong and healthy he is — a female lion will choose her mate by the look of his mane.

## Horns

Animals use horns to fight, to dig, to work — or just to show off! Some female animals will even pick a mate because his horns are the biggest. A rhinoceros beetle uses its horns to flip other beetles in a fight and to dig into a safe hiding place.

## Shells

Shells protect animals' soft bodies from danger the way a helmet protects your head. Some animals, such as turtles and clams, can hide inside their shells. A turtle keeps the same shell throughout its life, but a lobster sheds, or molts, its old shells as it grows.

## Antennae

For some animals, antennae do the jobs that our five senses do for us. Antennae can hear an insect's wings flapping nearby, smell danger in the air or taste a flower. A butterfly can even tell the location of the sun with its antennae!

## Wings

Wings allow animals to fly away from predators or travel long distances. High up in the air, these animals have a bird's-eye view of the ground below, helping them to find food and homes. Some bats use their wings like a blanket by folding them around their bodies!

## Fangs

Fangs are long, sharply pointed front teeth. Animals use fangs to grab, kill and eat their food. Bears use their fangs to tear open logs to find ants and grubs. Some snakes and spiders have deadly venom in their fangs that can paralyze or even kill large animals.

## Scales

Scales protect an animal like a suit of armor. Although hard and bony, scales bend and slide so the animal can move easily. Snakes and chameleons shed, or molt, their old skin and scales, when they grow bigger.

## Spikes

Spikes make animals prickly so their enemies won't want to touch them — or eat them! A puffer fish's spikes can contain a deadly poison. A hedgehog, if attacked, will curl into a spiky ball that keeps away most predators.

## Flippers or fins

Flippers are like paddles, and fins work like the rudder of a boat. Flippers help animals move through the water. Fins help them balance and steer as they swim. Penguins also use their flippers to defend themselves and their young against enemies.

## Tentacles

Tentacles are like very long fingers. Squid have suction cups on their tentacles to help them grab small fish to eat. A star-nosed mole uses its twenty-two tentacles to navigate underground and hunt for food. Snails have small eyes on the ends of their tentacles!

To Luci-Anne and Stuart for all the extra fun they add to our family.

And special thanks to my editor, Yasemin, for trusting
me with this project! — H.T.

To Ben, for being the best — P.C.

Kids Can Press gratefully acknowledges the financial support of the Government
of Ontario, through the Ontario Media Development Corporation; the Ontario Arts
Council; the Canada Council for the Arts; and the Government of Canada,
through the CBF, for our publishing activity.

Published in Canada and the U.S. by Kids Can Press Ltd.
25 Dockside Drive, Toronto, ON  M5A 0B5

Kids Can Press is a Corus Entertainment Inc. company

www.kidscanpress.com

The artwork in this book was digitally rendered in Adobe Photoshop.
The text is set in Alghera.

Edited by Yasemin Uçar and Jennifer Stokes
Designed by Julia Naimska

Printed and bound in Malaysia in 9/2016 by Tien Wah Press (Pte.) Ltd.

CM 17  0 9 8 7 6 5 4 3 2 1

**Library and Archives Canada Cataloguing in Publication**

Tekavec, Heather, 1969–, author
Different? Same! / written by Heather Tekavec ; illustrated
by Pippa Curnick.

ISBN 978-1-77138-565-7 (hardback)

1. Animals — Juvenile literature.  2. Pattern perception — Juvenile
literature.  I. Curnick, Pippa, illustrator  II. Title.

QL49.T49 2017     j590     C2016-902575-6

## Antennae

For some animals, antennae do the jobs that our five senses do for us. Antennae can hear an insect's wings flapping nearby, smell danger in the air or taste a flower. A butterfly can even tell the location of the sun with its antennae!

## Wings

Wings allow animals to fly away from predators or travel long distances. High up in the air, these animals have a bird's-eye view of the ground below, helping them to find food and homes. Some bats use their wings like a blanket by folding them around their bodies!

## Fangs

Fangs are long, sharply pointed front teeth. Animals use fangs to grab, kill and eat their food. Bears use their fangs to tear open logs to find ants and grubs. Some snakes and spiders have deadly venom in their fangs that can paralyze or even kill large animals.

## Scales

Scales protect an animal like a suit of armor. Although hard and bony, scales bend and slide so the animal can move easily. Snakes and chameleons shed, or molt, their old skin and scales, when they grow bigger.

## Spikes

Spikes make animals prickly so their enemies won't want to touch them — or eat them! A puffer fish's spikes can contain a deadly poison. A hedgehog, if attacked, will curl into a spiky ball that keeps away most predators.

## Flippers or fins

Flippers are like paddles, and fins work like the rudder of a boat. Flippers help animals move through the water. Fins help them balance and steer as they swim. Penguins also use their flippers to defend themselves and their young against enemies.

## Tentacles

Tentacles are like very long fingers. Squid have suction cups on their tentacles to help them grab small fish to eat. A star-nosed mole uses its twenty-two tentacles to navigate underground and hunt for food. Snails have small eyes on the ends of their tentacles!

To Luci-Anne and Stuart for all the extra fun they add to our family.

And special thanks to my editor, Yasemin, for trusting
me with this project! — H.T.

To Ben, for being the best — P.C.

Kids Can Press gratefully acknowledges the financial support of the Government
of Ontario, through the Ontario Media Development Corporation; the Ontario Arts
Council; the Canada Council for the Arts; and the Government of Canada,
through the CBF, for our publishing activity.

Published in Canada and the U.S. by Kids Can Press Ltd.
25 Dockside Drive, Toronto, ON M5A 0B5

Kids Can Press is a Corus Entertainment Inc. company

www.kidscanpress.com

The artwork in this book was digitally rendered in Adobe Photoshop.
The text is set in Alghera.

Edited by Yasemin Uçar and Jennifer Stokes
Designed by Julia Naimska

Printed and bound in Malaysia in 9/2016 by Tien Wah Press (Pte.) Ltd.

CM 17 0 9 8 7 6 5 4 3 2 1

**Library and Archives Canada Cataloguing in Publication**

Tekavec, Heather, 1969–, author
Different? Same! / written by Heather Tekavec ; illustrated
by Pippa Curnick.

ISBN 978-1-77138-565-7 (hardback)

1. Animals — Juvenile literature. 2. Pattern perception — Juvenile
literature. I. Curnick, Pippa, illustrator II. Title.

QL49.T49 2017     j590     C2016-902575-6